Little Prickles

Written by Kate and Gavin Nelson
Illustrated by Gavin Nelson, Kate Nelson, and Layne Suhre

To Nana, Papa, and Tía, with love

Kate and Gavin have written and illustrated books for the Kids Are Authors Competition
since third grade. Their book *The Music Inside Me* was the Grand Prize Winner
for Fiction in 2005. They are thrilled and honored to have *Little Prickles* join
The Music Inside Me as a Grand Prize Winner.
Their cousin, Layne Suhre, helped them to illustrate *Little Prickles*. They hope that the
Kids Are Authors Competition continues to inspire kids to write as much as
it has inspired them. Kate and Gavin are seventh grade students at
The Montessori Middle School in Norwalk, Connecticut.
Layne Suhre is a seventh grade student at Lake Bluff Middle School in Lake Bluff, Illinois.

Meet the Authors

Gavin Nelson

Kate Nelson

Layne Suhre

Little Prickles the porcupine cried to his mommy, "No one likes to play with me! I'm too prickly! I hate my sharp, pointy quills."

"Oh, my dear Little Prickles, you need your quills to keep you safe," his mommy said softly. "One day, they may come in handy, and I think your quills make you look quite handsome," said Mama Prickles.

So, Little Prickles went off to another lonely day at school.

Nobody would tag him when they played tag. Ouch!

Nobody would go on the slide with him. Ouch! Ouch!

He never got tapped for duck-duck-goose. Ouch! Ouch! Ouch! Other kids weren't ducks or geese, and they got tapped!

He wished he never had quills — even Stinky the skunk was more fun to play with. At least he didn't hurt.

So, he sat and sulked and was very, very grumpy. When Speedy the turtle asked if he wanted to go swimming, Little Prickles just grumbled, "Go away, I'm too prickly."

And when Slimy the salamander asked if Little Prickles wanted to play on the swings, all Slimy heard was, "Go away, I'm too prickly."

And when Quackers the duck asked if he wanted to play checkers, the answer once again was, "Go away, I'm too prickly."

He answered them all without ever looking up in his grumpy, grumpy voice.

One day at school, Mrs. Hoot was teaching them how to write the alphabet. "The best way to write well," said Mrs. Hoot, "is to have a nice, thin, sharp stick. If any of you have toothpicks at home, they work very well. You just dip the stick in ink and…."

"Wait!" screeched Little Prickles. "I have tons of nice, thin, sharp quills that would work perfectly."

"But you need those to keep you safe, Little Prickles," reminded Mrs. Hoot.

"But I have soooo many. It's okay, Mrs. Hoot," said Little Prickles.

So, everyone crammed around Little Prickles — but not too close — and one by one they each pulled out a quill. Little Prickles beamed from ear to ear.

At home that night, Mama Prickles asked, "Little Prickles, what happened to your quills? It seems like some are missing."

"Oh, Mama, it was the best day at school! I gave everyone a quill to write with! They came in handy just like you said!" he exclaimed.

"That wasn't quite what I meant by handy, Little Prickles. Your quills are an important part of you. They're what make you *you*!"

The next morning at school, Little Prickles heard, "I broke my quill. Can I have another?"

"I lost my quill. Can I have another?"

"My mommy wants one!"

"My daddy wants one."

"My sister wants one."

And so, one by one, Little Prickles gave away more and more and more quills until...

he had only three quills left!

By the time Mrs. Hoot arrived at the classroom, she gasped. "Little Prickles, what has happened to all your quills?" she asked with a trembling voice.

"I gave them away to all my new friends!" Little Prickles blurted out happily.

"You did what?" stammered Mrs. Hoot. "But Little Prickles, look at your nice, pink skin. You're a very tasty meal for a hungry fox now."

In all his happiness at having new friends, Little Prickles hadn't realized just how few quills he had left! He swallowed a big lump in his throat.

He sat by himself and felt scared and sad. Mrs. Hoot was right. Without his quills, he was a nice tasty treat for a big, mean animal. Without his quills, he didn't feel like a porcupine. Without his quills, he didn't feel like himself anymore. Two big tears spilled down his cheeks.

Mrs. Hoot saw his tears and spoke softly to the class, "Little Prickles was very kind and generous to give everyone quills and more quills, and even more quills. He shared little parts of himself with all of you." Mrs. Hoot turned to Little Prickles and said, "You don't need to give away everything that is important to you to be liked. You can be liked for who you are, quills and all."

"But nobody likes me, Mrs. Hoot," cried Little Prickles.

The class looked confused. Goggles the raccoon spoke up. "It wasn't your prickly quills that we didn't like. It was because you were always so grumpy. When we asked you to play, you always grumbled, 'Go away, I'm too prickly.'"

"I thought nobody wanted to be near me," muttered Little Prickles.

Buzzy the bee chimed in. "Being a bee isn't easy either. I have a stinger that can hurt, too, but there are still lots of games that I can play with my friends. We may not want to get too, too close to you, but we'd still like to be your friend."

"You would?" asked Little Prickles.

"Yes! Yes! Yes!" yelled the whole class.

Little Prickles could not stop the huge grin that appeared on his face. It felt much better to smile than to be sad and grumpy.

"Now what are we going to do with you, Little Prickles?" asked Mrs. Hoot, looking at his big, pink tummy.

Little Prickles' classmates knew exactly what to do. From that day on, they promised to keep Little Prickles safe until his new quills grew back. Every day, they formed a circle around Little Prickles and walked him all the way home to safety. And Little Prickles happily joined in all the games he could play with his friends.

It took a while for Little Prickles' quills to grow back. When he looked like a porcupine again, Mama Prickles said, "Little Prickles, I have something for you." She plucked a quill from her side and said, "Take this and use it wisely. Every time you write with it, remember it's what makes you special."

Little Prickles carried the quill carefully to school, and on the top of every paper he wrote, "I am Little Prickles, quills and all."

Kids Are Authors®
Books written by children for children

The Kids Are Authors® Competition was established in 1986 to encourage children to read and to become involved
in the creative process of writing.

Since then, thousands of children have written and illustrated books as participants in the Kids Are Authors® Competition.

The winning books in the annual competition are published by Scholastic Inc.
and are distributed by Scholastic Book Fairs throughout the United States.

For more information:
Kids Are Authors®; 1080 Greenwood Blvd.; Lake Mary, FL 32746
Or visit our web site at: www.scholastic.com/kidsareauthors

ISBN 10: 0-545-11967-7

ISBN 13: 978-0-545-11967-2

12 11 10 9 8 7 6 5 4 3 2 1

Cover and Book Design by Bill Henderson

Printed and bound in the U.S.A.   First Printing, July 2008